Pedro the Amazon Rainforest Parrot and Friends

Short Stories, Fuzzy Animals and Life Lessons

Karma for Kids Books

Norma MacDonald

Pedro the Amazon Rainforest Parrot and Friends
Short Stories, Fuzzy Animals and Life Lessons

Copyright © 2018 Norma MacDonald

First Edition

Published by: Find Your Way Publishing, Inc.
PO BOX 667
Norway, ME 04268 U.S.A.
www.findyourwaypublishing.com

ISBN-13: 978-1-945290-27-5

ISBN-10: 1-945290-27-7

Printed in the United States of America.

Dedication

This book is dedicated to all the people trying to make the world a better place. Keep going! You are making a positive difference!

"When you wake up every day, it's like a new birthday: it's a new chance to be great again and make great decisions."
~ Poo Bear

Table of Contents

About This Book

Welcome to our Karma for Kids Book Series. We are very grateful that you picked up this book. We believe that together we can make a positive difference, one child at a time. In a recent survey, more than 70 percent of U.S. adults said that they think people are ruder now than they were 20 years ago. The Karma for Kids Book Series gives hope to this recent concern.

We strive to instill important life lessons in the lives of young children. We are firm believers that we reap what we sow and think that if this simple lesson is taught to children at a young age, their lives have the potential to be absolutely amazing.

We once knew a dog named Karma. She was a beautiful, Labrador retriever. It wasn't until after she passed, at 11 years old, that we realized just how fitting her name really was. Karma is indeed a retriever.

Whatever we threw out, Karma was always happy to

bring it back to us. It didn't matter what it was, she always brought it back. If we threw out an ugly, stinky, dirty sock she'd bring it back without question. If we threw out a sweet smelling, beautiful bouquet of flowers she'd bring it back. It's the same in life. Whatever you send out, is what you will get back, guaranteed, every time. Our Karma for Kids Book Series hopes to instill this easy-to-understand lesson into the lives of children at a young age. God, the Divine Source, the Universe, wants to bring you all that your heart desires, and it will, effortlessly. But first, you've got to "throw out" what you want it to bring back to you, so that it can! We get what we give. Have fun with this and then watch your life unfold in amazing ways. God bless!

Find all of Norma MacDonald's Karma for Kids Books at Amazon.com.

For more of our Karma for Kids books please visit us at:

www.findyourwaypublishing.com

Other books that we recommend to help children succeed in all areas of their lives:

Can Camels Dance? Short Stories, Fuzzy Animals, and Life Lessons by Norma MacDonald

Arctic Adventures: Short Stories, Fuzzy Animals, and Life Lessons by Norma MacDonald

Kyle Kitten and Friends: Short Stories, Fuzzy Animals, and Life Lessons by Norma MacDonald

The Panda Family Relies on Each Other: Short Stories, Fuzzy Animals, and Life Lessons by Norma MacDonald

Matt the African Meerkat and Friends: Short Stories, Fuzzy Animals, and Life Lessons by Norma MacDonald

Kimmie Koala and Friends: Short Stories, Fuzzy Animals, and Life Lessons by Norma MacDonald

Cranky Crocodile Saves the Day: Short Stories, Fuzzy Animals, and Life Lessons by Norma MacDonald

The Many Adventures of Peppy the Emperor Penguin: Short Stories, Fuzzy Animals, and Life Lessons by Norma MacDonald

Lucy Llama and Friends: Short Stories, Fuzzy Animals, and Life Lessons by Norma MacDonald

Ethan Eagle and Friends: Short Stories, Fuzzy Animals, and Life Lessons by Norma MacDonald

Billy Brown Bear and Friends: Short Stories, Fuzzy Animals, and Life Lessons by Norma MacDonald

Humble Heron and Friends: Short Stories, Fuzzy Animals, and Life Lessons by Norma MacDonald

Peter Penguin and Friends: Short Stories, Fuzzy Animals and Life Lessons by Norma MacDonald

Alexei the Siberian Tiger and Friends at the Circus: Short Stories, Fuzzy Animals, and Life Lessons by Norma MacDonald

Guaranteed Success for Kindergarten; 50 Easy Things You Can Do Today! by Marrae Kimball

Guaranteed Success for Grade School; 50 Easy Things You Can Do Today! by Marrae Kimball

The Secret Combination to Middle School: Real Advice from Real Kids, Ideas for Success, and Much More! by Marrae Kimball

High School Success: How to Create Your Own Path, Beat Anxiety and Depression, Master Your Goals and Dreams by Marrae Kimball

Would you please consider leaving a short review for our books, online, because they help us spread the message! Children deserve the very best that life has to offer. Reviews don't have to be long, a few sentences will do, and they help more than you know! Thank you!

Pedro the Amazon Rainforest Parrot and Friends

Short Stories, Fuzzy Animals, and Life Lessons

Karma for Kids Books

Norma MacDonald

Chapter One

Imagine living in the world's largest tropical rainforest—the Amazon. This big and beautiful forest in South America is filled with thousands of different kinds of birds, thousands of different kinds of fish, and millions of different creepy, crawly bugs. There are over 10,000 different kinds of birds in the world and approximately 50 percent of that number live in the Amazon.

The Amazon rivers and trees are also home to super scary creatures like meat-eating fish called piranhas, electric eels, poison dart frogs, jaguars, and loads of poisonous snakes.

Because the trees in the rainforest are so tall and thick with leaves, the ground below is always damp and dark. But high up in these lush trees live some of the world's largest and most colorful birds. Also known as parrots, these birds live in the Amazon rainforest and are called Macaws.

These beautiful birds like to talk a lot and have very loud voices. The rainforest has lots of yummy food that the macaws like to eat. They love to fill up their bellies with fruit, seeds, leaves, flowers, and nuts. Their large beaks are so strong that they can even open hard coconut shells! These amazing birds are often found at the local clay cliffs licking the rocks. This helps the bird's tummies to stay healthy.

Macaws can live for 60 years or more! And they really enjoy hanging out together. Six friends have been playing together since they were little. Their names are Armando, Evora, Leonardo, Nadalia, Pedro, and Kiania. All of them have a special gift. Each one of them can make their voices sound like the calls of one of the other animals in the rainforest. They have been practicing these calls since they were young. They like to use their imitation voices to confuse others or make them laugh.

Armando can call out like a howler monkey. Howler monkeys have great big bodies and really big voices. They can be heard from very far away. Armando's voice isn't quite so loud. Armando can screech out like a howler monkey, but the truth is, he is very afraid of howler monkeys. He tries to stay as far away from them as possible. That's hard to do where he lives because the rainforest is filled with them. Howler monkeys aren't the only things that Armando is afraid of.

Armando's friends sometimes like to fly to faraway places to hang out by the Amazon river and watch the humans who fish there. They also love to watch the river dolphins, especially when the dolphins are playing. Armando wants to join his friends, but flying far from his nest makes him nervous. He likes to stay close to home.

His friends want to help him. One morning they gather around and try to encourage him to join them for the day. "You don't have to be afraid," says Kiania. "We will all fly together, and you can be in the middle. We'll all protect you."

"That won't help," Armando says. It's not that he is afraid to fly alone. He flies by himself all the time when he's hungry or when he's trying to get away from the howler monkeys.

Pedro is eager to get going. "If we leave now, I promise we'll be home before dark. Lots of birds are afraid of the dark."

"It's not that," says Armando.

"Are you afraid we'll get lost?" asks Evora, who has gotten lost many times.

"It's not that," Armando shakes his bright green head. "I can always find my way back home."

"Then what is it? Why are you afraid? Do you think we won't find enough to eat by the river?" asks Leonardo who is always thinking about food.

"No. No. No!" squawks Armando. "I don't know why I feel scared, but I do. So, it's just better if you go without me."

Kiana wants to stay and keep Armando company. But she also wants to go to the river. "I can't make up my mind," she says. "What do you think, Armando? What should I do?"

Armando doesn't want Kiana to miss out on the fun trip. "Go," he says. "I'll be fine. Don't worry about me."

His friends are sad, but they don't know what else to do. So they fly off together towards the river without him. A tear falls from Armando's eye as he watches them go. He would love to be flying to the river together with his friends, but something inside of him always holds him back. He doesn't understand it.

No one else in his family has this problem. In fact, he doesn't know of any other bird who is afraid to fly far from home. Armando feels so alone.

He thinks about the good time his friends will have at the river. That makes him feel even worse.

A group of howler monkeys are screeching and they seem to be coming closer. Armando has learned their warning call and he screeches it out as loud as he can. The cry of danger makes the monkeys head in a different direction.

Armando is hungry. He thinks about the yummy fish his friends will eat. He feels too sad to go look for food by himself. So, he stays in his nest. He starts to feel very, very sorry for himself. His head drops to his chest.

"What's the matter with you?" a voice cries from a close by tree.

Armando squints his eyes and spots his old friend, Karlos the Kingfisher. The green bird has a long-beak and an orange and white chest which makes him easy to see. Armando motions him to come over to his nest.

"You hungry?" asks Karlos.

Armando nods.

"There are a whole bunch of fish in the creek over there. Let me go fetch you a couple, okay?"

After Armando eats, he feels a lot better. Karlos perches on a branch near Armando's nest. "Talk to me, amigo. Tell me your troubles, my friend."

"It's this stupid fear thing," says Armando. "I'm afraid to fly far away, like to the river, and I don't understand why."

Karlos sits and thinks for a bit. "Did this fear come all of a sudden, or have you always been afraid to fly far from home?"

Armando thinks back to when he was little. "I guess I have always been scared. It was worse when I first learned to fly. I never wanted to leave the nest. My parents had to force me."

"That's very interesting," says Karlos. "What is the farthest you have flown?"

Armando points. "Just to the other side of the creek, where those big rocks are."

"You've never gone beyond them?"

"Nope."

Karlos waits a minute then offers a suggestion. "How about you try to fly just a little further each day or once a week. Whichever is better for you. Once you are comfortable with that distance, pick a point a bit further away and fly there. A little each time. What do you think?"

Armando shivers a bit. "I don't know. Makes me nervous just thinking about it."

"How about we try it together?" asks Karlos. "Pick a spot just beyond the rocks. Not too far. I will be right beside you."

Armando agrees and the two birds take off towards the rocks on the other side of the small creek. It takes them about ten minutes to get to the rocks. They stop and rest for a few minutes. "Whenever you're ready," says Karlos. "Pick a tall tree and we will fly to it together."

"But not too far, right?" asks Armando, his voice shaking a bit.

"You choose," says Karlos.

So, Armando picks the tallest tree which is not terribly far from the rocks. He takes a big breath and takes off with Karlos at his side. Three minutes later they land on one of the large branches. "Are you okay?" asks Karlos.

Armando's bright green feathers are quivering, and his heart is pounding, but his eyes beam with happiness. "I did it!"

Karlos spreads out his wings and gives him a pat. "Congratulations!"

Once he calms down, Armando looks for another destination. "Where to next?"

"Not yet, amigo. I think maybe we should fly back to your nest and tomorrow you can fly to this tree again. Keep doing it until you feel comfortable, then pick another spot, further away."

Armando agrees. "Thanks, Karlos. You've been a big help."

"It's nothing," says Karlos.

The two birds spread their wings and fly back to Armando's nest. It takes another week before Armando is able to fly beyond the tallest tree. He is able to go a little further every week. Three months later, much to their surprise, Armando is able to join his group of friends for an outing to the river where they laugh and play. Everyone is surprised and happy, especially Armando. And he can't wait to do it again!

Chapter Two

Pedro is a lovely rainbow-colored parrot who likes to imitate the sounds of all the different kinds of frogs and toads of the rainforest. He can croak the voices of the bright-colored poison dart frogs, tree frogs, the see-through glass frogs, giant cane toads, and the large smooth-sided toads. His special talent makes his friends laugh and laugh and laugh.

Pedro has many friends, but sometimes his friends get angry with him. That is because he doesn't like to wait. In fact, Pedro hates to wait. He doesn't like it when his friends are late. He won't wait one minute for anyone. "Being late is rude," he always says.

Waiting to eat is another problem for Pedro. When he's hungry, he wants to eat right away. And he especially hates to wait when he plans to take a fun trip. It always seems like the day, to go, will never, ever come.

"You are the most impatient bird in the entire rainforest!" Pedro's father often says to him.

But Pedro doesn't think that being impatient is a problem. No matter how many times his friends and family try to encourage Pedro to be patient, he just doesn't listen.

"The problem is because of everyone else," he says. "If others could just be on time, we wouldn't have to wait for them. Dinner time is 6 o'clock. Why should we ever have to wait any longer?"

One of the chores Pedro's parents gave him is to pick up his little brother from parrot preschool every day at noon. The preschool usually lets out on time, but sometimes the young parrots come out a little bit late. Today is one of those days.

Pedro perches on a tree outside of the school. His tummy is growling already. He didn't eat any breakfast this morning because he was in a hurry to meet his friend, Leonardo, and couldn't wait a minute longer for his mom to put his food on the table.

It is already five minutes past noon and the preschoolers have not yet been let out of their classroom. Pedro flaps his wings and shifts from one foot to the other. He doesn't want to wait one more minute. But if he leaves now, who will bring his little brother home?

Pedro looks around and notices his friend, Evora, who is waiting for her little brother, too. Evora and Pedro live close to one another. They are neighbors. Pedro has an idea. He calls out to Evora. "Hey! Do you think you could bring my little brother home? I can't wait any longer."

"Sure. No problem," says Evora. "I'll bring him straight home."

"Thanks," says Pedro as he takes off from the branch and heads home.

As soon as he arrives at the family nest his mom asks him where his little brother is. He explains that Evora is bringing him home. "Where's lunch?" he asks.

His mother puts his food in front of him. "Your impatience is going to lead to big trouble someday. You shouldn't have left without your brother. Isn't Evora that parrot that always gets lost?"

"Well, um, kinda," says Pedro gulping down a mouthful of nuts. "But she knows the way to our house. No problem."

A half an hour later, Evora and Pedro's little brother still haven't arrived. Pedro's mom is worried. "Where could they be?" she asks.

"Maybe school let out really late today. I'm sure they are fine." Pedro says. "Don't worry."

But his mom couldn't sit and wait around any longer. "I'm going to Evora's house to see if her parents have heard anything."

Another hour goes by. His mother has not returned. Pedro is starting to feel nervous. Where are his mother and little brother? Maybe something bad has happened. If his little brother is missing, it will be his fault because he didn't wait for him. "Maybe mother is right," he says to himself. "I should be more patient. I should have waited for my little brother. I shouldn't have left without him."

Pedro promises himself that in the future he will try really hard to be better about waiting. All he wants now is to see his mother and little brother again. He paces back and forth along a large branch, watching for them.

Finally, he spots two colorful birds flying towards him. It is mother and little brother! Pedro is so relieved. "What happened? Where did you find him?" asks Pedro as soon as his family lands.

"Evora invited me to eat lunch at their house because she was afraid her mom would be worried if they didn't come straight home since school let out so late," explains Pedro's little brother.

"But I asked Evora to bring you home," says Pedro. "You should have come straight home." Pedro looks at his mom. "Are you going to punish him for not coming home?"

"Why should I punish him for what you did? If you hadn't been in such a hurry to get home, this wouldn't have happened. If only you would've waited a few more minutes. It was your responsibility but because of your impatience you passed it off to someone else. If anyone needs punishment, I think it's you, Pedro."

Pedro lowers his head in shame. "You're right. I've been thinking about that. I need to learn to wait. I need to be more patient. But how?"

"I used to have the same problem when I was young like you," says Pedro's mother. "Your grandmother taught me a few things that have helped me. Would you like to know what they are?"

"Please," says Pedro. "Tell me."

"What has helped me most," his mother says, "is to find something to do while I am waiting. For example, you could whistle a song or practice your frog and toad imitations. You could think happy thoughts or stretch and breathe. It's important to learn to trust that everything happens in perfect timing. Once you learn these easy tools, you'll find the time flies by."

"Those are good ideas," says Pedro. "I will try."

Pedro's mother pats him on the shoulder with her wingtip. "I know you will become a patient bird one day. It takes practice but don't give up, you will get it."

"Thanks, Mom," Pedro says. "I hope so, and I can't wait to start practicing."

Chapter Three

Leonardo loves to eat. He wakes up hungry and goes to bed at night feeling hungry. No matter how many berries and nuts he eats, he never seems to be able to get enough food to make him feel full. He often worries that he won't be able to find enough food to eat, so every day he collects extra food and stores it in a hole in the tree where he lives. He has been putting nuts in that hole for over a year and it is almost full to the top.

Today, Leonardo stretches his unique white wings and flies from his nest especially early so that he can be the first one of all the macaws to find the ripest berries and nuts. Most of the rainforest animals are used to seeing his bright yellow body early in the morning flying back and forth to his nest with a beak full of food.

Leonardo's first stop is to check for the yummiest berries. But this morning, the best bushes are empty. Ripe or not ripe, there is not one single berry. Leonardo checks all of the berry bushes in the area and they are all the same. Empty! The hungry macaw cocks his head in confusion. This has never happened before. His stomach growls. Who could have come? Leonardo is always the earliest bird. He decides it is time to move on to the nut trees. Certainly, the nut trees will be full of nuts. It is nut season.

The first tree Leonardo reaches, the one that usually has the most nuts is completely bare. He rubs his eyes. He can't believe what he is seeing. The day before yesterday this tree was loaded with nuts, but today there is not a single nut in sight. What could have happened? Leonardo's heart is thumping like a wild drum in his chest. He quickly flies to the next nut tree. And the next. And the next. Every single nut tree is completely empty!

By this time, many of the other birds of the rainforest have woken up and are on the hunt for their breakfast. The birds begin to twitter and squawk in alarm. There's no food! No berries! No nuts! No food!

As fast as a raging river flows during rainy season, the news of the food shortage spreads throughout the thick green forest. The sound of all the birds of the rainforest chirping all at once is ear-piercing. The other animals join in and before long, even the nocturnal animals, who normally sleep during the day, are wide awake. "What's happening?" they ask.

The rainforest buzzes with the energy of the animal's nervous excitement. Everyone is asking the same questions. Does anyone know who came in the night and stole all the nuts and berries? Did anyone see or hear anything?

The answer is no. It is a mystery. No one can explain it. And the biggest, most important question on all the animal's minds is—what are we all going to eat today? And tomorrow? And what about the next day?

Leonardo is worrying more than anyone. He has stored up a bunch of nuts in a hole in the tree where his nest is. He won't starve. But he is worried that some of the other birds will come and ask him for his food and then he will have to share it. So, he stays very quiet and keeps his private food stash a secret. He is hungry, but he doesn't want anyone to see him eat his nuts. So, he waits until it starts to get dark and hopes no one is watching as he sneaks into his stash and starts chomping on a beak full of nuts. But someone is watching. More than just one someone. A group of little ones perch on a limb above.

"Do you have food?" asks a tiny voice.

"Will you give us some?" asks another.

"We are very, very hungry," says another small voice.

The group of little birds' eyes drip with sad tears. Their heads hang low. "Please," they say together. "Just a couple of nuts. That's all. Our tummies hurt."

Leonardo looks at their tiny beaks, mouths open, and sighs. He really doesn't want to share his food, but their sad, hungry faces touch his heart. "I guess I can give you a couple of nuts. Just this once."

The small birds chirp their thanks and fly away with joyful faces. For the first time in his life, Leonardo actually feels happy to have been able to share his food. His heart feels full. But still, he hopes that the little group of young birds will be the only ones to visit his tree. After all, he can't feed everyone!

Before he goes to sleep, Leonardo sings like a river dolphin. It is his favorite imitation. And it usually keeps all the other birds away. Once he is sure everyone is asleep, he sneaks back to his storage hole and eats until his tummy is so full he feels it will burst. He falls asleep thinking about the next day. Will there be food to be found?

Leonardo wakes up to a flurry of flapping wings and chirping; it's so loud he has to cover his sensitive ears. When his eyes adjust to the bright morning sunlight, he shakes his head in disbelief. Every single branch and twig of the tree he lives in has a bird perched on it! Hundreds of hungry eyes stare at him with mouths open. "We're hungry. We heard you have food. Please give us some!"

Leonardo's heart starts to beat very fast in his chest. What can he do? These birds will eat all his nuts and then there will be nothing left for himself. He has worked hard for a year to get his storage hole full. It will all be gone in one day. Then what will he eat? What if there are no nuts to be found ever again?

The chirping and squawking of the birds gets louder and louder. They move closer and closer to his nest. They crowd around him as he blocks the entry to his storage hole. What is he to do? He can't keep them away, so he moves aside. "Go ahead. Eat! But please just take nuts for yourself so there will be enough for everyone."

Less than an hour later, the last bird has taken away the last of the nuts. Leonardo didn't even get a single nut for himself. But before long, the hundreds of birds gather around Leonardo's nest and sing a special beautiful song of gratitude. "We will never forget this day and what you did for us," they sing. "Thank you for sharing your food, Leonardo. We have heard that a group of hungry bears has been eating the food. But there is more food on the other side of the mountain. Plenty. It is further away, but we will help you gather more nuts and refill your tree in no time."

Leonardo's heart swells with joy. Instead of being sad that his food is all gone, he feels super happy that he could share with others. Leonardo now knows that generous giving creates happiness all around.

Chapter Four

It takes a couple weeks before the food problem in their area gets better. Thankfully the trees and bushes filled back up with nuts and berries and the problem disappeared. But there are always other dangerous things for the macaws of the Amazon rainforest.

One of the biggest dangers to the macaws, throughout the world, is the bird catcher. Many people want to own macaws of their own as pets. So, there are people who go into the wild to catch them, so they can sell them. The macaws know that being caught is a terrible thing. They have heard that if they are captured, they will be taken far from their home and far from their friends and families. Being caught means being put in a small cage for the rest of one's long life. All alone with very little freedom. That is a very scary thing.

Nadalia doesn't worry too much about being caught by bird catchers. She knows what the traps look like and she believes she will never fall into one. Every morning she wakes up and preens her red body. She pays special attention to fixing the feathers in her bright blue and yellow wings. She loves that her feathers are so many different colors. She believes macaws with many colors are more beautiful and smarter than the dull one-colored parrots. For example, Armando, who is all green, is afraid of everything. Sure, she thinks, he flies to the river now, but he is still afraid of a lot of other things. So silly she thinks to herself.

Nadalia wishes all the macaws were multi-colored like herself and all her friends. She thinks the rainbow parrots are the best at imitating the calls of other animals. Everyone says that Nadalia can sound just like a spider monkey. She can also sound like a dozen other animals. She doesn't know any of the plain, one-colored macaws who can even come close to her skills at imitating other animals.

Nadalia and a group of her rainbow-colored macaws have planned a trip to the Iguazu Falls. This is the most beautiful group of waterfalls and trees and the birds just love to go there. They like to perch in the trees close to the falls and call out to each other in all their different voices. The air is fresh and misty with water and they often meet other macaws from different parts of the rainforest there. It is so much fun!

At the end of this especially exciting day, Nadalia and her friends are tired but happy. The flight home takes about an hour, so they decide to leave before the sun starts to dip below the tops of the trees. Nadalia has made a new friend from a different part of the forest and they enjoy chatting together so much that she doesn't want to go home quite yet. "You can leave without me," She tells the others. "I will be fine. I'm not one of those silly birds who gets lost," she says.

And that is true. Nadalia doesn't get lost, but she runs into an even bigger problem than losing her way.

Nadalia's favorite thing to eat is mango. It can be hard to find, so right away when she spots a lone mango she swoops down to grab it. Sadly, she doesn't notice that there is something quite strange about that mango and she is not careful. Eager to fill her belly, Nadalia is pecking away at the mango when suddenly her feet swing out from under her and she is pulled up into a thin rope trap.

She cries out and flaps her wings in a frantic attempt to escape. But the ropes that bind her just get tighter and tighter. Nadalia's little heart pounds in her chest. What is she going to do? She looks all around to see if there is a human bird catcher approaching, but she doesn't see anyone. Maybe she still has time to escape. She tries to bite at the ropes, but they are very strong.

Looking up, she notices a bird flying in her direction. "Help!" she cries in her loudest voice. "Please help me!"

The bird comes closer. It is a plain blue macaw. He recognizes Nadalia and remembers that she is the parrot who always puts her beak in the air and refuses to talk to him. "Looks like you've got yourself in quite a mess," he says.

Nadalia is so happy to see another bird, she doesn't even care that he is a plain colored one. "Help me get out of this trap," she says. "And hurry!"

"Oh," says the bright blue parrot, looking around. "You're speaking to me?"

"Of course, I'm speaking to you," she says, trying her best to put on her sweetest voice. "Can you please do something to get me out of this?"

The blue bird cocks his head to one side and stares closely at the rope that is wrapped around

Nadalia's foot. He sees what he needs to do to free her, but he doesn't say anything.

"Don't just stand there," Nadalia says with impatience. "Do something!"

The blue bird stays silent.

"You really are dumb. Don't you realize how much danger we are in?" she asks.

"Danger we are in? You seem to be the one in danger, not me."

"Stop talking and get me out of this trap, you dummy."

The blue parrot sighs. "So, it's true. You think you're smarter than me because you are more colorful, don't you?"

Nadalia doesn't say anything.

"Well, if you are so much smarter than me, why is it that you are stuck in a trap and I am not?"

Nadalia doesn't know what to say. For the first time in her life, she needs help from someone who she thinks is beneath her. She feels embarrassed, but she really, really, really must get out of this trap. "I'm sorry," she says, and lowers her head. "Maybe I haven't been as nice to you as I should have been. I'm sorry. I promise to do better if you will just help me. Please!"

The blue parrot has a good heart, and even though Nadalia has hurt his feelings in the past, he still feels sad for her and is happy to help.

"Of course, I will help you. But I hope this helps you realize that everyone is special, and strong, and smart in their own way, even if their feathers are plain and not as colorful as yours are."

Five minutes later, he has loosened the thin ropes and set her free. Nadalia thanks him. "I truly am grateful for your help," she says. "I was wrong about one-colored parrots. Again, I'm sorry. And I'm looking forward to getting to know you better, if you'll let me."

From that day forward, Nadalia widens out her wings of friendship to all macaws, especially the solid-colored ones. Because of this, she makes heaps of wonderful new friends, and is very thankful.

Chapter Five

The jaguar is one of the most dangerous big cats of the rainforest jungle. All the animals run or fly or swing through the trees to get away when they hear the snarl of a jaguar.

Evora has spent many hours perfecting her jaguar imitation. Sometimes she scares her friends with that loud cry, but she doesn't do it because she is mean. Evora knows that the voice of the jaguar is a good protection if she or her friends are threatened by one of their enemies. All the animals are afraid of jaguars. That's why she keeps practicing her jaguar call. She knows that someday it could save her life and her friends, too.

Sometimes Evora gets so busy with her voice training, she doesn't pay much attention to what is going on around her. That's what happens the day she and her friends go to the river. Evora doesn't hear her friends calling her when they decide to head back home. Pedro, who doesn't like to wait for others, urges the other macaws to leave without her. "I know we could wait patiently for her, but I think she will be fine. She'll find her way home on her own."

But Evora's closest friend Kiania doesn't agree. "You know Evora gets lost a lot. Don't you think we should wait for her?"

Pedro ruffles his feathers. "You can wait for her if you want. But I'm flying home now. Besides, she's not answering our calls, so maybe she headed back already."

The others are tired and agree with Pedro. Kiania has a hard time deciding what to do. She doesn't want to leave her good friend, but she also knows her family will be nervous waiting for her to arrive at their cozy nest. At the last minute, she joins the group and heads for home.

A little while later, Evora looks around and realizes all of her friends are missing. She flies around for a while, and then asks some of the kingfishers if they've seen the macaws.

"They left about a half an hour ago," says one of the fishing birds.

Evora's heart starts to beat a little faster. How is she going to get home? She never pays much attention to the way to and from the river because she doesn't need to. She's always flying together with her friends.

She asks the kingfishers if they know which direction she needs to go to get back home and they point with their wings towards the sun. Evora thanks them and starts flying towards the sun. But the bright rays in her eyes are a big problem. She decides to wait until the sun has set a bit to continue her journey. She knows home is not too terribly far away and she can get there before the forest goes completely dark. She hopes, that is, if she doesn't get lost.

Once the sun has dipped down below the horizon, Evora can't figure out exactly which direction she should go. She starts to panic. "I'll never get home. I'll be lost in this strange part of the rainforest forever. What am I going to do?" she asks herself.

As the forest grows darker, Evora's fear gets bigger. To protect herself, she starts growling like a jaguar. This makes her feel better, but she still is afraid that a real jaguar will find her and eat her for dinner. She keeps up the jaguar calls until her throat grows hoarse and she can barely utter a sound. She flaps her wings a few times and sighs. "I'll never get home tonight.

Just then, a friendly owl flies near her and asks, "What are you doing here? Shouldn't you be home by now? It'll be darker than dark before too long."

Evora explains that she is lost and describes to the owl the area where she lives. "I'm terrible with directions. Do you think you could help me find the way back to my nest?"

"Sure," says the friendly owl. "I know just where that is. We'll be there in a jiffy. Follow me!"

They fly off together and before the darkness has overtaken them, Evora spots the tree where her family has lived for years. Before the owl leaves, he gives her a suggestion. "Have you ever thought about using a map?"

Evora doesn't know what a map is, so the owl explains it to her and says owls are great mapmakers. Feeling relieved and tired, she settles safely into her nest just as the deep darkness fills the skies. She falls into a deep, deep sleep.

In the morning, a voice awakens her from sleep. It's her friend Kiania. "I am so glad to see you made it home. I was so worried about you!"

Evora tells her friend the story of how she got lost and how the owl helped her get home. "You would think I'd know my way around by now," she says. "I'm not a silly baby bird anymore."

"I wonder if there's something you can do about this getting lost problem?" Kiania asks.

"The owl, who helped me home, suggested someone could make a map for me."

Kiania cocks her head to one side. "What's a map?"

"It's a drawing that shows where things are. Maps show rivers, creeks, mountains, and things like that. The owl said her cousins are great at making maps. I am going to meet with them later today. I hope they can make me a good map. I hope it will help."

And so Evora meets with the mapmaking owls. She flies away from them with a great map in her beak and hope in her heart.

The map brings Evora great success. Whenever she loses her way, she perches on a tree and unrolls the map. After looking around and comparing what she sees with what is shown on the map, she is able to decide which way to go.

Sometimes the other birds tease her because she always flies with a map in her beak, but she doesn't care. The most important thing is that Evora never loses her way home again!

Chapter Six

Kiania wakes up early one morning, stretches her wings, and watches the mist rise off the tops of the tall trees. "What should I do today?" She remembers that she promised her grandmother she would gather nuts first thing in the morning for a special cake. She also told her little brother that she would teach him how to imitate the songs of the famous Musician Wrens.

As is true for most, the life of an Amazon rainforest macaw is full of choices. Everyday Kiania must make up her mind about things, like what to eat, where to go, who to play with and when to rest. Most of the parrots have no problem making up their minds, but for Kiania every decision she has to make causes her trouble. "What if I make the wrong choice and something bad happens?" she often asks herself.

As she is thinking about what to do, Evora and Nadalia fly up and land on the branch beside her. "We are going to the river; do you want to come?"

Kiania hasn't been to the river in a long time and she really wants to go, but what about the promises she made to her grandmother and little brother? "Let me think about it," she says. "Can you come back in a half an hour and I will let you know?"

"Sure," say her friends. "We are going to go find something to eat. We will be back in a little bit."

Kiania's two friends have just left when Armando lands in the tree next to her. "What are your plans for the day?" he asks.

"I am not sure yet," she says. "What are you doing?"

"Today I was supposed to go exploring with Leonardo, but he had to cancel. You wanna go exploring with me?"

Kiania loves exploring, but what about all the other things she promised to do today? And what about going to the river with Evora and Nadalia? "Can I let you know soon?" she asks.

"No problem," says Leonardo. "I will come back soon."

Leonardo leaves and Kiania sits and thinks about what she is going to do. She really wants to go to the river, but she would also love to go exploring. Maybe she could teach her little brother those songs tomorrow or the day after. But then what about grandmother? Maybe she would have time to gather the nuts for her before she went to the river. Or would she rather go exploring? Too many choices!

Kiania cannot make up her mind, so she just stays perched on the branch of the tree and does nothing. Before long, Evora and Nadalia return. "Are you ready to go to the river?" they ask.

"I don't know. I want to go, but I have other things I have to do today. I'm afraid if I go to the river, my grandmother and little brother might be mad at me. Maybe I could go talk to them really quick. What do you think I should do?" she asks.

Her friends are not surprised. They know Kiania well and they know she has a hard time deciding what to do. They could wait all day for her to make up her mind. But they don't want to make decisions for her. "We are going to go now. You can either come with us or stay here. Your choice."

But Kiania cannot choose. So, they leave without her. "Maybe another day," they shout as they fly toward the river.

Kiania watches them go. She feels sad. Why can't she ever make up her mind? Before long, Leonardo is back. "Ready to go exploring?" he asks.

"I don't know what to do," she says. "I want to go with you, but I made promises. I will go talk to grandmother and my little brother and then I can let you know."

Leonardo shakes his head. "By then it will be too late to go exploring. I will go ask someone else. You and I can go another time. No worries."

When her friend leaves, Kiania feels even sadder. So, she goes to find her grandmother. But when she arrives, her grandmother is already making the special cake. "Where did you get the nuts?" asks Kiania.

"You didn't come, so I sent your sister to get them."

"I'm sorry, Grandmother," says Kiania. "I promise I will gather twice as many nuts next time."

Kiania hugs her grandmother and flies off to find her little brother. No one has seen him. Finally, she sees her father and asks him if he knows where her little brother has gone.

"He went exploring with Leonardo," says her father.

Kiania lets out a big, long sigh. She started the morning off with so many options, but she has missed the opportunity to do any of them. Now she doesn't know what to do. So, she flies back to her favorite perch. Her belly rumbles. She realizes that she hasn't had any breakfast. "I should have asked grandmother for something to eat," she thinks. "Maybe if I go back her special cake will be ready." But then she thinks maybe it would be better if she just went quickly to the berry bushes and eat there instead. Or maybe she should look for something else. It is just so hard for her to decide!

While she is thinking about what to eat, she starts to feel sleepy. If she just takes a little nap, maybe then she will be able to decide what to do about breakfast.

It feels like she has only been asleep for a few minutes, but when Kiania wakes up, the sun is high in the sky. Lunch time already. By this time, her tummy is feeling sharp hungry pains, so she flies straight to her grandmother's nest. But she is not home. She flies to the closest berry bushes, but they are empty.

Finally, she takes the shortest path to her parent's home. By now she is so tired and hungry that she tumbles into their nest.

"What's wrong, Kiania," her mother says. "You don't look so good."

"Hungry," she says in a soft weak voice. "Haven't eaten today."

When her tummy is full, her mother asks her what she has been doing. "Were you too busy to eat breakfast this morning?" she asks.

Kiania shakes her head. "I didn't actually do anything this morning."

"What happened?" she asks. "I thought you had plans."

"Nothing worked out," Kiania explains to her mother about all the things that happened that morning. "I couldn't make up my mind. And by the time I got to grandmother's, I was too late. Why is it so hard for me to make decisions?"

"Your uncle was just like you when he was young. He was always missing out on fun things to do because he couldn't make up his mind."

"What helped him?" Kiana asks. "Seems like he doesn't have trouble making decisions anymore."

"He had to learn not to think too much and not to be afraid to make mistakes. And he learned to talk to others."

"So other people could make the decisions for him?" Kiania asks.

"No," her mother says. "Everyone has to make their own decisions. Learn to trust yourself. Your uncle learned to ask good questions to help him decide quickly. Knowledge helps. They say that those who make decisions quickly are the most successful in life. Finally, we all had to remind your uncle he needed to just do something."

"And all that really can help?"

"Yes. Just go with the first thing that pops into your head and then stick with it. Make a decision and then make the decision right. Try it. For example, what would you like to eat for dessert? Mango or banana?"

Kiania likes both fruits. At first, she has a hard time deciding, but then she just picks one. "I'll have a banana."

"Good job," her mother says. "Was that really so hard to do? You made the decision, and now you can make the decision right by enjoying the banana."

Kiania smiles. "I think, with a little practice, I can become better at making decisions."

"I know you can," says her mother. "And the more you do it, the easier it will become."

Will You Help Us Out?

Would you please consider leaving reviews online for our books because they help so much? They don't have to be long and will only take a minute. It would mean a lot and help us get the word out, to other children, as well. Thank you so much! We are extremely grateful.

AFTERWORD

Thanks again for picking up this book! You are participating in making our world a better place to live and grow. When children learn that they will always get back what they give, they will start to navigate their lives in incredible ways. When you give a smile, and make someone's heart feel lighter and happier, you can be sure that you will receive something in the near future that will make your heart happier as well. When you do something kind for someone, you can be sure that someone will do something kind for you in the coming days ahead. It's truly amazing how it works! Have fun with it and enjoy!

For more of our *Karma for Kids Books* please visit us at:

www.findyourwaypublishing.com

Find Norma MacDonald and her books online at Amazon.com.

Can Camels Dance? Short Stories, Fuzzy Animals, and Life Lessons

Arctic Adventures: Short Stories, Fuzzy Animals, and Life Lessons

Kyle Kitten and Friends: Short Stories, Fuzzy Animals, and Life Lessons

The Panda Family Relies on Each Other: Short Stories, Fuzzy Animals, and Life Lessons

Matt the African Meerkat and Friends: Short Stories, Fuzzy Animals, and Life Lessons

The Many Adventures of Peppy the Emperor Penguin: Short Stories, Fuzzy Animals, and Life Lessons

Kimmie Koala and Friends: Short Stories, Fuzzy Animals, and Life Lessons

Cranky Crocodile Saves the Day: Short Stories, Fuzzy Animals, and Life Lessons

Lucy Llama and Friends: Short Stories, Fuzzy Animals, and Life Lessons

Ethan the Eagle and Friends; Short Stories, Fuzzy Animals, and Life Lessons

Billy Brown Bear and Friends; Short Stories, Fuzzy Animals, and Life Lessons

Humble Heron and Friends; Short Stories, Fuzzy Animals, and Life Lessons

Peter Penguin and Friends; Short Stories, Fuzzy Animals, and Life Lessons

Alexei the Siberian Tiger and Friends at the Circus: Short Stories, Fuzzy Animals, and Life Lessons

Other books that we recommend to help children learn important life lessons:

Guaranteed Success for Kindergarten; 50 Easy Things You Can Do Today! by Marrae Kimball

Guaranteed Success for Grade School; 50 Easy Things You Can Do Today! by Marrae Kimball

The Secret Combination to Middle School: Real Advice from Real Kids, Ideas for Success, and Much More! by Marrae Kimball

High School Success: How to Create Your Own Path, Beat Anxiety & Depression, Master Your Goals & Dreams by Marrae Kimball

Again, thank you for reading and sharing this book! YOU are making the world a better place. Would you please consider leaving a short review for our books, online, because they help us spread the message! Children deserve the very best that life has to offer. Reviews don't have to be long, a few sentences will do, and they help more than you know! Thank you!

All children deserve a chance at a successful and happy life.

If you have ideas for stories, please feel free to share and send them to:

Melissa Eshleman
Find Your Way Publishing, Inc.
PO Box 667
Norway, ME 04268
Melissa@findyourwaypublishing.com

www.findyourwaypublishing.com

Thank you!

Disclaimer

www.ingramcontent.com/pod-product-compliance
Lightning Source LLC
Chambersburg PA
CBHW020639130626
46552CB00003B/1313